LASSIE
COME-HOME

LASSIE

COME-HOME

by ERIC KNIGHT

Abridged by FELIX SUTTON

Illustrations by HANS H. HELWEG

1976 Printing
ISBN: 0-448-02139-0
Library of Congress Catalog Card Number: AC 66-10899

GROSSET & DUNLAP · *Publishers* · NEW YORK

EVERYONE in Greenall Bridge knew Lassie. In fact, you might say she was the best-known dog in the village.

One reason was that the village people agreed she was the finest collie they had ever laid eyes on.

There was another reason why Lassie was so well known. It was because, as the women said, "You can set your clock by her."

That had begun four years before, when Lassie, who was owned by Sam Carraclough, was a bright, harum-scarum yearling. One day Sam's boy, Joe, had come home bubbling with excitement.

"Mother! I came out of school today, and who do you think was sitting there waiting for me? Lassie! Now how do you think she knew where I was?"

Whatever it was, Lassie was waiting at the school gate the next day, and the next. And the weeks and the months and the years had gone past, and it had always been the same. Women glancing through the windows of their cottages, or shopkeepers standing in the doors on High Street, would see the proud dog go past on a steady trot, and would say:

"Must be five minutes to four—there goes Lassie!"

The whole village knew that the Duke of Rudling, who lived in a great estate and had kennels full of fine dogs, had been trying to buy Lassie for three years. But Sam had stood his ground.

"It's no use raising your price again, Your Lordship," he would say. "It's just—well, she's not for sale—not for any price."

"I NEVER WANT ANOTHER DOG"

One day Joe had come out of school with the others and gone to the gate where Lassie always waited. But Lassie was not there!

Joe looked up and down the street. Perhaps Lassie was late! He knew that could not be the reason, though, for animals are not like human beings. Humans have watches and clocks. But animals need no machines to tell time. There is something inside them that is more accurate than clocks. It is a "time sense," and it never fails them. They know exactly when it is time to take part in some well-established routine of life. Joe knew that. But where could Lassie be? Joe ran home to tell his mother.

"Mother! Something's happened to Lassie! She didn't meet me!"

As soon as he had said it, Joe knew something was wrong.

"Ye might as well know it right off, Joe," his mother said. "Lassie won't be waiting at school for ye no more."

"Why not? What's happened to her?"

"Because she's sold. That's why not."

"Sold!" the boy cried. "Sold! What did ye sell Lassie for?"

"Now, she's sold, and gone, and done with," his mother said. "Let's say no more about it."

Mrs. Carraclough looked at her son, then put her plump arm around him. "Look, Joe, ye're getting to be a big lad now, and ye can understand. Ye see—well, things aren't going so well for us these days. We've got to have food on the table, and we've got to pay rent—and Lassie was worth a lot of money and—well, we couldn't afford to keep her, that's all."

Young Joe did understand. He knew what "poor times" were. He knew that the Yorkshire coal mines were shut down. He knew that his father no longer went to work.

Yet his heart still cried for Lassie. And he asked one question.

"Couldn't we buy her back some day, Mother?"

"Now, Joe, she was a very valuable dog and she's worth too much for us. But we'll get another dog some day. Just wait."

Joe bent his head and shook it slowly. His voice was only a whisper.

"I never want another dog. Never! I only want—Lassie!"

AN EVIL-TEMPERED OLD MAN

The Duke of Rudling stood by a hedge and glared about him.

"Hynes!" the Duke boomed. "Hynes! Where is the man?"

As the Duke shouted his name, Hynes, the kennelman, came into view. "Coming, sir," he said. "Coming."

"Look here, Hynes," the Duke said. "I want you to see a new dog I've just bought. Finest collie I've ever laid my eyes on."

The Duke and Hynes went down the path to the kennels. And there, by the mesh-wire runs, they halted, looking at Lassie lying inside.

The Duke clicked his tongue in signal to the dog.

"Come, collie! Come over here! Come!"

For just a second, the great brown eyes of the collie turned to the man. Then they turned back to mere empty staring.

"Keep an eye on her, Hynes," the Duke said. And he turned away.

When he was gone, the dog lay unmoving in the sunshine. Then, as the shadows began to lengthen, she arose and started pacing back and forth along the wire. The time sense began to grow stronger in her.

Suddenly, Lassie knew what it was she wanted.

LASSIE COMES HOME AGAIN

When Joe came out of school and walked through the gate, he could not believe his eyes. He stood for a moment, and then his voice rang shrill. "Lassie! Lassie!"

He ran to his dog, and buried his face deep in her rich coat. He stood again and almost danced with excitement. "Come, Lassie," he said.

He raced on down High Street, and Lassie ran beside him, leaping high in the air, barking a sharp cry of happiness.

Then suddenly Joe slowed down. He knew the truth. His father had not bought the dog back again. Lassie had escaped! That was it!

And so young Joe walked slowly as he turned up the hillside street to his home. By his door he turned and spoke to the dog sadly. "Stay at heel, Lassie," he said.

He opened the door and walked in.

"Mother," he said. "I've got a surprise. Lassie's come home."

Joe's words raced on. "I was coming out of school and there she was. Right at the gate waiting for me. I could see she was homesick for us—for all of us. So I thought I'd bring her right along, and we could just . . ."

"No!" It was his mother, interrupting loudly. "No! She's sold! Now take her right back to them that's bought her."

Joe turned to his father sitting before the fire. "Ye know, Father, happen they don't care for her right, up at the kennels. I'll bet you anything they're not feeding her right."

"By gum," his father said. "She does look a bit poorly. But the minute she's fed, she goes back."

Mr. Carraclough warmed a pan of food and set it before the dog. And he and his son stood watching Lassie eat happily. It was Mrs. Carraclough who seemed to remember first that Lassie no longer belonged to them.

"Now, please," she cried. "Will you get that dog out of here?"

She paused, and they all listened. There was a sound of footsteps coming up the garden path. Then the door opened and Hynes came in. His eyes turned to the dog before the hearth.

"I thought so!" he cried. "I just thought as how I'd find her here!"

Joe's father rose slowly.

"I was just feeding her," he said. "Then I was off to bring her back."

"I'll bet ye were!" Hynes mocked. "Well—it just so happens that I'll bring 'er back myself—since I happened to drop in."

Taking a leash from his pocket, he walked quickly to the collie and slipped the noose over her head. And Hynes and Lassie were gone.

THE HIDING PLACE ON THE MOOR

The next day Lassie lay in her pen. As the afternoon deepened, she began to stir. Suddenly she lifted her head and scented the breeze. Then she got up and began walking about the pen, walking round and round. Then in one corner she halted, and clawed at the wire.

As if that were the signal, Lassie suddenly understood her desire. It was time! Time to go for the boy!

She pawed at the wire but made little impression. Memory told her that she had escaped there before by tearing at the wire, then digging and squeezing underneath. But Hynes had cut off that path to escape. Frantically, she reared and stood on her hind legs against the wire, looking up.

If you couldn't go under a thing, you might go over it!

She leaped and fell back. She leaped, and leaped, and leaped again.

Finally, Lassie turned back the length of her pen and raced in a running start. This time her hind legs found some support in the angle of the fence. She struggled higher and her front paws reached the top. For a second she hung there. And then, slowly, she pulled herself upward.

She launched herself out and dropped to the ground outside the pen. She was free!

A few hours later, Hynes beat loudly on the cottage door and walked in without waiting for an answer. "Come on, where is she?" he demanded.

Mr. and Mrs. Carraclough stared at him, and then their glances turned toward each other.

"So that's why he's not home!" Joe's mother said.

"Aye!" her husband agreed.

"They're together—him and Lassie. She's got away again and he's afraid to come home. He knows we'll take her back."

Sam rose slowly. Then he went to the door.

"Now don't thee worry, lass," he said to his wife. "Joe'll not have gone far. Just up to the moors he'll head."

Sam's face was stern.

"You'll just go right home, Mr. Hynes," he said. "Thy dog'll be back to thee, just as soon as I find her."

Then Sam went out into the dark evening. He went up the hill until he reached the great, flat tableland that stretched, foreboding and bleak, for mile after mile over the Yorkshire country. As Sam's feet stepped upon the first echoing stones, he heard the sharp bark of a dog. He followed the sound. And there, in the lea of a huge rock, he found his son and the dog.

"Come, Joe," he said.

Obediently the boy rose, and in miserable silence he followed his father. Lassie walked at his heel.

When they were near the village again, his father spoke once more.

"Go right home, Joe," he said. "I'm taking her back to the kennels."

The next morning, after the family had finished breakfast, Sam took his son to a battered bench under a giant oak tree that shaded the cottage.

"Joe," he said, "ye know ye did wrong, lad. Don't ye?"

"Aye, Father. I'm sorry."

"I know. But being sorry afterwards doesn't help at the time, Joe. Ye see, a chap's got to be honest. And sometimes, when a chap don't have much, son, he clings to being honest harder than ever—because that's all he's got left.

"It's like this, Joe," his father went on. "Lassie is sold and that's all. We've taken the Duke's money, and now she belongs to him."

"But, Father, she might run away again . . ."

"Nay, lad nay! She'll never run away again—never no more!"

"What—what did they do to her?" asked Joe.

"Well," his father said, "when I took her back last night, the Duke got angry at me and Hynes and the whole lot. And I got mad at him, and I said if she got away again he'd not see her no more. And he said if she ever got away again, I was welcome to her. But he said he'd see she didn't.

"So he's taking her up to his place in Scotland to get her ready for the dog shows. Hynes has gone up wi' her. And she's never to be kept down here in Yorkshire no more. So bide it like a man, Joe, lad, and let's never say another word about it as long as we live."

"Father," Joe said. "Is it very far to Scotland?"

The man breathed deeply and sadly. "Aye, Joe," he said. "It's a long, long road. Much farther than you'll ever travel, I'd say. A long, long road."

THE LONG ROAD HOME

It is, as Sam Carraclough told his son, a "long, long road" from Greenall Bridge up into the Scottish Highlands.

More than four hundred dreary miles from the village of Greenall Bridge was the great Scottish estate of the Duke of Rudling.

It was there that Lassie found her new home.

There, she submitted patiently to the handling of Hynes. But each day, just before four o'clock in the afternoon, something waked in her. She would tear against the wire of her pen or dash at the fence and try to leap it. Lassie had not forgotten!

One day, weeks later, Hynes was taking Lassie for a walk. The leash was around Lassie's neck and she was going obediently at Hynes's heel.

Quite needlessly, Hynes tugged at the leash. "Come along!" he snapped.

Lassie felt the sudden tug and slackened her pace. Hynes tugged again on the leash. "Come on, when I tell yer!" he shouted.

Lassie backed away from the threatening tone. Hynes yanked again. Lassie braced herself for the tug and lowered her head. Hynes pulled harder, and the leash slipped over the dog's head. Lassie was free!

Hynes jumped to grab her, but instinctively, Lassie jumped away. "Here, Lassie," Hynes said. "Come here!"

Had it been any other time of day but four o'clock, Lassie might have returned to Hynes as he bade her. But she did not. One instinct told her to obey. But there was another impulse that stirred her. It was the time sense. It was time—time to go.

She wheeled and began trotting off. Behind her, she heard Hynes shouting. There was nothing to tell her that the appointment she was going to keep was four hundred miles away. Four hundred miles—but that would be for a man, traveling straight by road or train. For an animal how far would it be—an animal that must circle and sidetrack till it found a way? A *thousand* miles it would be—a thousand miles through strange country it had never seen before, with nothing but instinct to tell direction.

Lassie lifted her head and scented the breeze as if asking for directions. Then, without hesitation, she raced down the road to the south. The long journey home had begun.

It was growing late as Lassie, trotting slowly, came down the dusty road. In the last of the long northern twilight, two men sat outside a cottage. Suddenly, the older man pointed.

"Willie," he said, "see yonder, that fine dog comin' down the road."

"Aye! It looks like the new collie belongin' to the Duke," his companion replied. "It'll be escaped, no doubt."

"And there'll be a reward for the man that finds it!"

The younger man dashed into the street and barred the dog's way.

"Here, lass!" he called. "Here, lass!"

Lassie looked up at him. Her ear had caught the sound that was almost like her name: lass. Had the man walked toward her, she might have let him place his hand on her. But he moved too quickly. She was reminded of Hynes. She veered and ran past him.

As the man raced after her, Lassie broke into a steady gallop. The longer he chased her, the more firmly it was becoming fixed in her mind that she must not let any human being put his hands on her. Lassie had learned her first lesson. She must keep away from men.

For the first four days Lassie traveled without pause, resting only briefly during the nights. But then a new demand began to gnaw at her senses. It was the call of hunger. She had no trouble finding streams to quench her thirst. But food was different. All her life, food had been put before her on a platter. But now there was no one to feed her. Instinct would have to teach Lassie what to do.

On the fifth day, as she went along at her fast trot, her nose detected a warm, thick smell—the smell of food! Coming down the path was a weasel, and by his side he dragged the freshly killed body of a rabbit. When he saw Lassie, he bared his savage teeth in defiance.

Lassie had never seen such an animal before. The ruff on her neck rose. The lips curled back from her teeth. She sprang. But the screaming weasel flashed aside like lightning and disappeared into the heather.

Lassie sniffed at the warm smell of the rabbit that lay on the path. It smelled good. It was food.

After that, she had a newly acquired sense. As she traveled along, whenever her keen nose told her of the nearness of game, she became a hunter. She scouted and ran and caught it, and she ate. But she killed to live, and no more.

Weeks and many long miles later, Lassie came to the banks of a swift-flowing river. She was moving more slowly now, for the pads of her feet were bruised and sore, and in her left forepaw a thorn was festering.

Lassie looked at the white, tumbling water. Then she hurled her body far out into the stream.

The current caught her and tumbled her about, but she came to the surface and started swimming for the far shore. Often she was submerged in the swift eddies. But each time, as she came up, she was still fighting in the right direction.

As she finally neared the farther shore, a current swept her away and her body was driven cruelly against a rock. A stab of pain ran like fire along her side. The swift water drew her down and she disappeared.

In a backwater, Lassie's head broke the surface again. Fighting and swimming with all her force, she made the landing. Her feet touched ground. But the water that had soaked into her coat was almost too much of a burden. She staggered and her muscles seemed unable to support her.

At last she broke into a clumsy trot. The pain in her side and in her left forepaw did not come into her mind. She adjusted her gait as best she could to favor the injuries. It was long past nightfall when at last she denned up beside a field wall.

She lay close to the ground. She licked at her paw, trying with her tongue to reach between the pads where the thorn festered. For nearly an hour she worked, but in the end the thorn was still there. With a sigh like that of a tired man, she laid her head on her extended leg and closed her eyes.

It was not yet dawn when she awoke and tried to raise up. Her forequarters came from the ground, but her hindquarters would not move. During the night, the injury to her side had stiffened. In the last crash against the rocks in the river, she had broken a rib and badly bruised the muscles and joints of her hind legs. They had become completely useless.

Instinct told her that she could travel no farther. She must stay here. For days she lay, coiled and hidden away, her eyes bright with fever.

Then, on the afternoon of the sixth day, she lifted her head at last. Weakly, she licked her forepaw. Nature had done its work. From the festering sore, the thorn had worked its way out. Slowly she struggled to her feet. She limped across the field and hobbled downhill to where her nose told her there was water. She found the tiny stream, lowered her head and lapped. It was the first drink she had had for nearly a week.

Faintly, in the depth of her mind, the time sense woke again. It was time—time to go. Stiffly she crossed the stream. Going painfully and slowly, she struck out to the south. Lassie was on her way again.

LASSIE FINDS A FRIEND

Several nights later Lassie came through a field. She was going at a slow, painful walk. It took all her efforts to keep her legs moving. But she was still going south.

Across the meadow, she saw the lights of a house. Faintly, she smelled warmth and food. She stumbled on until she collapsed and lay on her side. Her eyes were glazed.

Inside the house, two old people sat before the fire. The man was reading and his wife sat in a rocking chair, knitting.

Suddenly she looked up. "Dan!" she said. "D'ya hear that? There's something by the chickens!"

"Now, now," the man said. " 'Tis nought but the wind."

The old woman spoke again. "There! I heard it again."

The man rose from his chair. "Now, now, Dolly," he said. "I'll go to make your soul content. I'll look around."

He took the lantern down and went out. But in a moment his voice came from the darkness. "Get your shawl and come," he cried. "I've found it!" It was Lassie, lying like a dead dog in a ditch beside the hedge.

"Poor, poor thing," the woman said. "Who would leave their dog out on a night like this?"

Her husband picked Lassie up, carried her inside and laid her on a rug in front of the warm fire. "I doubt it'll live till the morn," he said.

"Well, we can try, the poor beastie. Look at it shiver. It isn't dead. Get that sack fro' the cupboard and dry it off." She took a tin of condensed milk from the shelf, heated it in a pan on the grate, and began to spoon the warm liquid into Lassie's almost lifeless mouth.

Weeks later, Lassie lay on the rug, her ears erect. Strength had returned to her since she had been in her new home. And now the one driving force of her life was reawakened. It was the time sense. It always grew worse in the afternoons. As the clock moved round toward four, it became maddening. It was time—time to go for the boy!

Lassie rose and went to the door. She whined and lifted her head. She paced back and forth, back and forth.

An hour later, Lassie went back to the hearth rug. The time was past. She lay down and looked into the fire.

The old woman had grown to love the beautiful collie, and she hoped the dog would be content with the snug little world of the cottage. But, at last, she realized it was no use to hope.

One afternoon, as Lassie lay stretched out on the rug, the woman spoke. "Dan," she said to her husband. "Dan—she's not happy here. These last three days she's not been eating. Every afternoon she walks, window to door, till I'm thinking she'll wear a path deep in the floor. She's going somewhere. She was on her way, and she got tired and she stopped here to stay till she got rested. But now she's better, and she wants to be on her way."

The old man did not answer. But when the time neared four o'clock, and Lassie rose, his eyes followed her. "Well, all right," the old man said.

His wife nodded. They both got up and the woman opened the door. Side by side, they followed Lassie out into the road. The woman's aged voice came clearly: "It's all right, collie. If ye must go, away wi' ye!"

Lassie caught the word "go." It was what she wanted. She turned and trotted off—straight across a broken field. Lassie was going south again.

Back on the road, the old woman stood and waved her hand. "Good-by," she said. "Good-by, collie—and good luck to ye!"

JOURNEY'S END

Joe Carraclough had last seen Lassie in the late spring. But spring had turned to summer, and summer to fall. And now the snow lay white and deep over the Yorkshire moors.

Joe still hoped for a miracle. He hoped that some day his dog would be there, waiting for him by the school gate. He knew that such a wonderful miracle could not possibly happen. But still he hoped.

Yet on this winter's day, coming across the schoolyard, Joe could not believe his eyes. There, walking the last few yards to the gate was—his dog!

But what a dog this was—no prize collie with fine coat glowing, with eyes alert and ears lifted proudly over the slim, proud head. This was a dog whose head and tail were dragging in the snow. She was crawling, rather than walking, and each step seemed a separate effort.

At last, she came to her old place by the school gate and, like a good dog, she lay down.

Joe raced across the schoolyard and fell to his knees beside her. He dug his hands deep into the scrawny fur that was matted with burrs and thorns and he cradled her drooping head in his arms.

Many evenings later, there came a caller to the Carraclough cottage. It was the Duke of Rudling.

As the door opened, Joe ran to Lassie, who was lying by the fire, and threw his arms about her. "This is not yer dog!" he cried. "No dog could come all the miles fro Scotland! This is not Lassie. It's another dog—yer dog's not here!"

Gently the Duke spoke to Joe's mother: "What's the lad talking about? What dog o' mine's not here?"

Now in dog-dealing the spoken word is a binding contract. The Duke looked long at Joe. Then he looked at Lassie, and he smiled.

"If ye mean that sad-looking dog that lies yonder," the Duke said, "why, that's not my dog.

"No, lad," the Duke said, "that's no dog o' mine. 'Pon my soul and honor, she never belonged to me."

The Duke turned and started out the door, muttering under his breath: "Bless my soul! I wouldn't ha' believed it! Four hundred miles!"

In the doorway, the Duke stopped. "Almost forgot why I came," he said gruffly. "Sam, you got a job?"

"Well," Joe's father said, "no—not exactly."

"That's fine," the Duke growled. "I need a man to run my kennels. Had to sack Hynes. And ye look like a man who knows dogs. The job pays seven pounds a week—and ye'll live in the cottage on the estate. I'll expect ye bright and early Monday morning."

With that, the Duke walked out and slammed the door. As he went down the path he chuckled to himself: "For five years I've sworn I'd have that dog on my place. And now, by George, I've got her!"

That evening, for the first time in many long months, Joe's father and mother were happy.

But Joe forgot them. He sat on the floor and held his dog close to him. "Ye're my Lassie," he crooned. "Ye're my own Lassie Come-Home!"